TOO Small Tola

and the Three Fine Girls

TOO Small Tola

and the Three Fine Girls

ATINUKE

illustrated by
ONYINYE IWU

CANDLEWICK PRESS

Dedicated to Solomon. Never forget—those
who are small can also be MIGHTY.
A

To my little bean, in the hope that you love these
stories and drawings as much as I do!
OI

Text copyright © 2021 by Atinuke
Illustrations copyright © 2021 by Onyinye Iwu

First US edition 2022
First published by Walker Books Ltd (UK) 2021

Library of Congress Catalog Card Number 2021953241
ISBN 978-1-5362-2517-4

22 23 24 25 26 27 LBM 10 9 8 7 6 5 4 3 2 1

Printed in Melrose Park, IL, USA

This book was typeset in Stempel Schneidler.
The illustrations were created digitally.

Candlewick Press
99 Dover Street
Somerville, Massachusetts 02144

www.candlewick.com

CONTENTS

Moji Grandmommy Tola Dapo

Tola Saves the Day

Tola lives in a run-down block of apartments in the megacity of Lagos, in the country of Nigeria. Tola's sister, Moji, is much cleverer than Tola. Tola's brother, Dapo, is much faster than Tola. And even short-short Grandmommy is taller than Tola. Which makes Tola feel so small-o!

It is a rainy Saturday. There is no school on Saturday. Tola, Moji, and Dapo are all at home.

But Grandmommy is not at home.
Grandmommy is out selling groundnuts by the
side of the road. That is her job. And her job
does not stop on Saturday. Her job stops only on
Sunday, for church.

In church Grandmommy wears her most
precious items—gold dangly earrings that are
kept on the shelf beside her bed. Those earrings
were worn by Grandmommy's own
mother and her grandmother and

her great-grandmother. When she wears them, Grandmommy recites all their names, thanking them for giving her strength to carry on.

Grandmommy says that she can feel their strength in her blood and in her bones. Moji used to say that this was unscientific—until she found out about DNA. Grandmommy was not surprised. She said scientists are only catching up with what people have always known.

But church day is Sunday. And today is still Saturday. So Grandmommy is not wearing her dangly earrings. She is at work. And although Tola and Moji and Dapo are not at school, and although they do not have jobs to go to, they still have work to do.

"You three must clean the rice," Grandmommy had told them.

Tola's family can only buy cheap sacks of rice. Cheap sacks of rice have many small stones in them, stones that must be picked out.

Selling groundnuts by the side of the road does not earn them enough to buy sacks of expensive clean rice.

And Grandmommy cannot earn the money for food and wash all their clothes and also clean the stones out of the rice. So Tola and Dapo and Moji have to help.

But in fact Moji is studying on the old computer that her scholarship school has lent her. She is frowning at the screen with her A+ frown.

And in fact Dapo is using his knees to keep a football up in the air. He is wearing his Africa Cup of Nations frown.

So in fact it is only Tola who is squatting on the floor picking stones out of the rice! From where she is, she can see the bed and the shelf with Grandmommy's gold earrings gleaming next to the Bible.

"Dapo!" she says to her brother. "You are supposed to be helping!"

Dapo kicks the ball up with his knees faster and faster and faster. Then he suddenly traps it under his foot like a rat under a broom. He beams at Tola.

"You see that?" he asks. "You see my World Cup moves? When I become a professional footballer, I will pay for somebody to pick the stones out of the rice." Dapo pauses.

"Do not worry, Too Small Tola. I will take care of you! But for now, I must practice!"

Dapo starts to kick the ball up on his knees again. And Tola rolls her eyes.

"Moji!" Tola says to her sister. "Come and do the rice with me!"

Moji raises her eyebrows at Tola.

"If I do the rice now, then I will not be able to study. And if I do not study, then I will not become a doctor. And if I do not become a doctor, then I will be picking stones out of rice for the rest of my life."

"But Moji—" Tola says.

"Leave me alone to become a doctor," Moji says. "Then I will buy us all expensive rice. Rice with no stones."

Moji turns back to her computer screen.

Tola scowls. She always does the Saturday jobs alone.

And picking stones out of rice takes forever.

And it is boring-o!

But Tola continues because if Grandmommy comes home and the rice is not finished, then she will not be happy. And Grandmommy might be small, but her lungs are not. And that is also why Tola never tells her that Moji and Dapo do not help with the Saturday jobs. Tola does not want to hear Grandmommy shouting, even if it is not at her.

Dapo kicks the ball up on his knees again. He makes a little grunt each time he does it.

"Dapo!" snaps Moji. "You are not allowed to do that inside! Grandmommy will be angry!"

But it is raining hard, so Dapo cannot practice outside. It is proper Nigerian rain, with fat drops flying down hard and fast like in a rich man's shower.

"And who will tell Grandmommy?" Dapo grunts. "You, who are supposed to be doing the rice?"

Moji glares at Dapo. Dapo keeps his eyes on the ball. Nothing can puncture his concentration! He is kicking faster and faster. And grunting faster and faster too.

"Dapo!" Moji shouts. "That ball will break something! And then what will Grandmommy do to you?"

It is Dapo's concentration that breaks! The ball rolls away and knocks into Tola's neat piles of rice and stones. They become one pile of rice and stones mixed together like before.

"Look what you did!" Tola shrieks.

"I told you!" Moji sings out.

"It was you!" Dapo shouts at her. "It was you who did it. You are a witch!"

"A witch!" Now Moji is shrieking too. "Who are you calling a witch?"

Tola sighs loudly and leaves them to argue. She is so angry she could box their heads together. But they look like they are going to do that themselves. So she leaves them to it and starts to separate the piles all over again.

Then
Moji remembers
that witch or no witch
she is supposed to be studying to become a
doctor. She flashes her palm at Dapo and turns
back to the screen with her A+ frown.

Dapo flashes his palm back. *Shame on you!*

The ball is resting in the corner of the room.
Dapo picks it up to practice again.

Moji shouts, "Go outside!"

"You want me to drown?" Dapo shouts back.

"What if your ball hits this computer?"

"You are just jealous!" Dapo accuses her. "You
know that footballers earn more money than
doctors!"

Dapo starts kicking the ball up on his knees
again.

"Anyway," he grunts, "I am not playing, I am studying."

"Studying!" Moji snorts.

"Yes!" Dapo grunts faster. "I am studying. You think you are the only one who can study?"

Moji sucks her teeth.

"Studying is hard," she says. "You, my friend, are just playing. Playing is easy."

Dapo stops. He holds out the ball to Moji.

"If you think it is easy, then you try," he says. "You try and see if it is not hard. Harder even than your studying."

Moji rolls her eyes and turns to the computer screen. Dapo laughs. He goes back to kicking the ball up on his knees.

"You see?" he grunts. "You are afraid."

Quick as a flash, Moji stands up and snatches the ball out of the air. She balances it on one knee. Tola watches. She watches to see if Moji is as good at football as she is at schoolwork.

11

Moji jerks her knee up in the air. Immediately the ball flies across the room. Tola freezes as she watches it sail over the bed toward Grandmommy's special shelf . . .

and hit it with a thump.

Tola cries out as if she has been hit herself.

Dapo groans as if he's been punched hard.

Moji is silent and still as a cockroach sprayed with Raid.

Grandmommy's Bible lands on the floor with a thud.

And the earrings fly up, up, up into the air. Tola covers her eyes.

When she uncovers them, Moji is scrabbling on her hands and knees on the floor. Tola holds her breath. Moji sits up holding one earring in her hand.

Tola starts to breathe again. And Dapo laughs a shaky laugh. Moji sighs with relief. With shaking hands she puts the earring back on its shelf. Then she goes back on her hands and knees.

Moji searches and searches and searches for the other earring.

She looks under the bed. It is packed with Grandmommy's boxes of old clothes and Sunday clothes and things that might one day be needed. Moji pulls the boxes out and looks in each one. But the earring is not there.

Then she empties all the buckets and bowls in the kitchen corner, just in case. Some have tomatoes in them. Some have onions. Some have tiny-tiny chili peppers. Moji spreads them all out on the floor. But the earring is not there.

Then she looks among all her books and files and papers on the crowded table. But the earring is still not there.

For a long time, nobody says anything. There are only the small sounds of Moji searching.

"I cannot find it!" Moji wails at last.

Her eyes are wide. She is breathing hard.

Immediately Dapo starts to search. This is not a time for quarreling, this is not a time for blaming, this is not a time for rivalry—this is a family crisis.

Dapo looks under the chairs and in the sack of rice.

"It must be here!" he mutters frantically.

But it is not.

He unrolls the mat he sleeps on and shakes it out.

"It must be here!" he mutters determinedly.

But it is not.

He moves Moji's piles of books and papers.

And Moji does not even complain.

"It must be here!" he mutters angrily.

But it is not.

At last Dapo wails, "Grandmommy will kill us. She will kill us."

"We must look more! We must look more!" Moji says frantically.

"Where?" Dapo asks, sitting back on his heels. "We have looked everywhere."

"We must look everywhere again!" Moji says. "Tola! Search the rice!"

Even though she knows it is not there, Tola does not argue. Slowly and carefully she searches through her piles of rice. How happy she would be if the earring were hiding safe among the grains. But it is not.

Dapo and Moji and Tola search and search until all hope is gone.

Tola looks out of the window. It is still daytime. Grandmommy will stay on her spot

on the Ikorodu Road selling groundnuts until night.

"There is still time," says Tola. "Still a long time to look."

So hopelessly Moji searches again under the bed. And hopelessly Dapo searches again on the table. And hopelessly Tola searches once more in her piles of rice and stones. But the earring is not there.

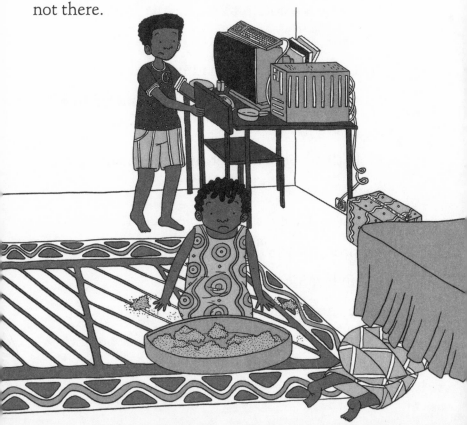

Moji lies on the floor looking at the ceiling.

"My school says that there are scholarships for doctors in Australia," she says.

Dapo sits hugging his knees.

"My coach says that China is looking for African players," he says.

Tola says nothing. She knows that Grandmommy might be short. But she can shout loudly enough to reach Australia or China when she is angry.

Then Moji says, "We had better do the rice. If we do the rice, then maybe Grandmommy will not be so angry."

Tola thinks that sometimes Moji is not as clever as she thinks she is.

"Maybe if we do the whole sack, then Grandmommy will not even notice that the earring is gone," Dapo says.

Tola thinks that Dapo is not clever at all.

Moji and Dapo jump up. Moji lights a

kerosene lamp. They squat by the sack and start to pick stones out of the rice so fast their hands are flashing.

Tola is lying under the bed where she has squeezed between the boxes to search for the earring. She is the only one small enough to fit there. She starts to wriggle out. And then she sees something glint. She squints. It glints again. In the tiny-tiny space between the heavy bed leg and the wall is something shiny.

Tola squeezes her little-little arm up between the boxes, toward the bed leg. Then she slips a tiny-tiny finger into the tiny-tiny space between the leg and the wall.

And her finger touches something smooth!

Tola hooks her finger around the smooth something and closes her hand around it. She draws her hand carefully back toward herself. Then Tola carefully opens her hand and looks. And there, resting on her palm, right in front of her eyes, is the gold earring.

Tola jumps up to shriek and bangs her head under the bed before her mouth can even open. Tola holds on to her head. She waits for the pain to stop.

And while she waits, her eyes fall on Moji and Dapo picking through the rice.

Those two never help her to do any Saturday job. Now look at them-o! Their hands are moving faster than a woman braiding hair!

Tola watches them. It is a pleasant sight to see them work hard. And as the earring is in her hand, all her worries are over. It is so pleasant that Tola continues to watch without saying anything.

And while she watches, Dapo and Moji frantically separate the stones from the rice. They forget to eat. They forget to drink. They work until the sun has reached the tops of the city's skyscrapers. They work until the sun has gone below the city's slums. They work so long that eventually Tola falls asleep.

In fact Tola wakes up only when she hears Grandmommy's heavy footsteps in the corridor outside the apartment. Tola wriggles out.

On the floor in front of her is a pile of stones. And all the rice is back in the sack.

Moji and Dapo have done it all! They have cleaned the entire sack-o!

Tola hears Grandmommy's hand on the door. Moji and Dapo are cowering behind the table. Behind them Tola quickly slips the earring back onto the shelf beside the other one.

The door opens. Grandmommy enters the room with her pans and brazier on her head.

She looks at Tola and Moji and Dapo and the pile of stones.

"Good evening, Grandmommy," Tola says.

"Good evening," says Grandmommy. "You have cleaned all the rice! Well done-o! Well done!"

Then her eyes narrow slightly.

"Moji?" she asks. "You are not studying?"

"No, Grandmommy," Moji says slowly.

"Are you sick?" Grandmommy asks.

"Maybe . . ." Moji says.

"Hmm," says Grandmommy suspiciously.

"Dapo?" she asks. "No football?"

"It is raining, Grandmommy," Dapo says.

"Raining?" Grandmommy looks out of the window at the clear sky.

"This morning," Dapo says. "It was raining this morning."

"Hmm," Grandmommy says again, even more suspiciously.

Then Grandmommy brings out three fresh
doughnuts from her basket. She holds them out
to Tola and Moji and Dapo.

"Take!" she says. "You must be hungry!"

Tola stretches her hand out and takes one
doughnut. Sugar sparkles on it!

"Thank you, Grandmommy!" she cries
happily.

Moji and Dapo stare at her. How can she be
so happy when the world is about to end?

"Moji, Dapo, nko?" Grandmommy asks,
surprised.

Moji and Dapo shake their heads. How can they eat doughnuts when the sky is about to fall down?

"I am not hungry, Grandmommy," Moji says.

"I—I cannot eat," says Dapo.

"You must be sick." Grandmommy frowns.

"I think so," says Moji.

Maybe Grandmommy will not be so angry if they are sick.

"Then you must have medicine!" Grandmommy says.

Moji's and Dapo's faces screw up. Grandmommy's medicine is so sour it makes the insides of a person's mouth stick together.

"Take! Take!" Grandmommy gives the other two doughnuts to Tola. Then she hurries around preparing the medicine.

Moji and Dapo look at the shelf. How long will it take Grandmommy to notice that one of her precious gold earrings is gone?

But on the shelf two gold earrings glow!
Dapo's mouth drops open. Moji's mouth
drops open too. And while their mouths
are open, Grandmommy pops a spoonful of
medicine inside each one.

Moji and Dapo splutter and gag. Then they
look at Tola.

Tola is looking at their doughnuts. She has already finished her own. Slowly she takes one bite out of each of her brother's and sister's doughnuts. Moji and Dapo splutter even more.

But is Tola not the one who has stopped the sky from falling down and averted the end of the world? She deserves all the doughnuts she can get-o.

Tola looks at them and then smiles her biggest and sugariest three-doughnut-eating smile!

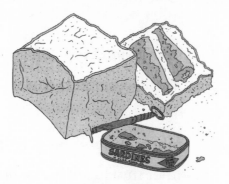

Tola Takes Control

Tola lives in a run-down block of apartments in the megacity of Lagos, in the country of Nigeria. In Lagos there are people who eat pizza, people who eat pepper soup, and people who eat suya and roasted corn. People who can eat morning, noon, and night.

Then there are people who work every hour of the day just to put bread and sardines on the table. People like Tola's grandmommy.

While Grandmommy is working, Tola and Dapo and Moji are at school. Tola and Moji are eager to go and are never late. But Dapo is often complaining and always in trouble.

"Come on, Dapo," Moji says. "Grandmommy is suffering by the side of the road so that we can go to school."

"But I am useless at school!" Dapo whines.

When Grandmommy hears him, she says, "You are useless at everything! You must try harder! Do you want to end up a street hawker like me?"

There is only one answer to that! So Dapo says nothing.

One day Tola wakes up. Something is different.

The cockerels are crowing. The room is getting light. She can hear Dapo snoring on his mat on the floor. She can hear Moji mumbling equations in her sleep. All that is normal, but still something is wrong.

Tola sits up. And there is Grandmommy, still in bed beside her!

Ah-ah! Grandmommy should have gone to

work long before dawn! She should be squatting over her fire, ready to sell groundnuts to people hurrying to work. Instead here is Grandmommy. Lying in bed. Her face covered with sweat.

Tola puts her hand on Grandmommy's arm. It is hot like fire.

"Grandmommy!" Tola cries.

Grandmommy does not even open her eyes. But Moji wakes up.

"Wa's it?" she asks.

"Grandmommy!" Tola sobs.

Moji sits up. She takes one look at Grandmommy's hot and sweating face and says, "Call Mrs. Abdul! Quickly!"

Tola jumps out of bed.

"Mrs. Abdul!" she shouts as she runs down the corridor.

Tola comes back with Mrs. Abdul hurrying behind her. Mrs. Abdul gives a loud cry when she sees Grandmommy.

Dapo wakes up. He blinks at everyone standing around the bed.

"Mama Mighty has a fever," says Mrs. Abdul. "A bad fever."

Dapo jumps up.

"Grandmommy!" he cries.

Grandmommy does not answer. Mrs. Abdul
looks at Moji.

"Have you checked her eyes?" Mrs. Abdul asks.

Moji nods. "They are OK," she whispers.

"Does she cough?" Mrs. Abdul asks.

Moji shakes her head.

"It must be malaria," Mrs. Abdul says.

Moji nods her head again. She is going to be a
doctor, so she knows.

Tola clutches her hands together. Malaria is serious! Dapo wails. He knows this too!

"Your grandmother needs medicine," Mrs. Abdul says firmly. "That is all."

"We have money!" Tola says.

She runs to where Grandmommy keeps her money. She pulls out the notes from the tin. "Is it enough for one of those bottles of medicine the herbal women sell from their baskets?"

Mrs. Abdul shakes her head. "Grandmommy is very sick," she says. "You will have to buy shop medicine."

Tola swallows.

"How much?" she whispers.

"Maybe five thousand naira," Mrs. Abdul says quietly.

Tola gasps. She is holding only two hundred in her hand. And that is all the money they have.

Moji stands up. "We will find the money," she says to Mrs. Abdul.

Tola and Dapo stare at Moji.

"I will be in my room," says Mrs. Abdul, going out.

Tola starts to cry. Five thousand naira! She has never before seen five thousand naira-o! What will happen to Grandmommy now?

Dapo is holding his head in his hands. Moji is wringing her hands.

"We could sell Grandmommy's earrings . . ." Moji whispers.

"No!" Tola cries immediately. "If we do that, Grandmommy's heart will break."

"But we have to get money." Dapo lifts his head. "Or . . ."

"Don't say it!" Tola closes her eyes tight. "Don't say it! And you cannot sell her earrings or all her strength will be gone."

"Then . . ." Moji bites her lip.

She is hopping from one leg to the other. Tola and Dapo look at her.

Suddenly Moji rushes to the wooden table. She pushes the flat tabletop off one of the legs. Then she puts her hand into the leg. It is hollow. And out of the hole Moji pulls a roll of money!

Tola and Dapo gasp loudly.

"Whose money is that?" Tola breathes.

"Grandmommy's," Moji whispers.

"Grandmommy's!" cries Dapo.

"But," says Moji, "she said we must never, ever spend it. Unless . . ." She stops.

"Unless what?" Tola asks.

"Unless Grandmommy was no longer here . . ." Moji whispers.

In the bed Grandmommy moans.

". . . and we were left alone," Moji finishes.

Moji and Dapo and Tola stare at one another.

"If we do not spend it on medicine, then soon we will be alone," Tola says slowly.

That would be worse, she thinks . . . than anything.

"We must use it to buy medicine!" Dapo says.

"So we are agreed?" Moji asks nervously.

Tola and Dapo nod vigorously.

And Moji gives the money to Tola. Tola is the best at counting.

Tola counts once. She counts twice. She counts three times.

"Along with the money in the tin, it will reach," Tola says.

"So take it-o," Moji says quickly. "Take it all and go to Mrs. Abdul."

Tola takes the money, gets dressed, and goes.

Mrs. Abdul ties baby Jide on her back. And together they leave the apartments.

Tola feels as shaky inside as the old danfo bus that they board.

She feels as cold inside as the shop that they enter.

She feels as small inside as the look in the pharmacist's eyes as she looks down on her.

But Tola hands over her money and takes the medicine. And prays it will work.

"Now she will get better," Mrs. Abdul says hopefully when they are back at the apartments and Grandmommy has had her medicine.

"It is well," says Moji in response.

"In'shallah," Mrs. Abdul replies, and leaves.

But it is not well, Tola thinks. Grandmommy is sick. And Tola is hungry. Hungry with no money and no food. They thought Grandmommy would work today and buy more.

"Moji?" Tola asks.

Moji is sitting on the bed next to Grandmommy. She is crying.

"Dapo?" Tola asks.

Dapo is lying on his mat with his face pressed down.

Tola looks at Grandmommy. If Grandmommy were well, she would say, "If we are hungry and the money is gone, then we must get more!"

Then she would tie her wrapper tighter, collect her pots and pans, and set off to work.

Tola looks at her sister and brother. Moji does not stop crying. And Dapo keeps his face pressed to the floor.

Slowly-slowly Tola gets up. Slowly-slowly she reties her wrapper. Slowly-slowly she piles Grandmommy's pans on top of her head.

Moji stares at her.

"What are you doing?" She hiccups.

"I am going to sell groundnuts," Tola says.

"Why?" Dapo asks.

"I am hungry," Tola says. "And we need money to buy food."

"But Grandmommy said that we would never become street hawkers!" Moji wails.

"Grandmommy cannot work for us now," Tola says softly. "So we must work for ourselves."

Moji cannot bear not to go to school. She looks at Grandmommy. She waits for her to say, "School is the priority. You three will never become street hawkers!"

But Grandmommy does not. She does not even open her eyes.

"O-ya!" Tola orders. "Moji, carry the sack of groundnuts! Dapo, carry the fire!"

Moji and Dapo stare at her.

Tola puts her hands on her hips.

"Maybe you two do not want to eat today?"

Slowly Moji stands up. She dries her eyes, reties her wrapper, and picks up the sack of groundnuts.

Slowly Dapo gets up from the floor, rubbing his own eyes. He puts on his shorts and picks up the brazier.

Together they go to ask Mrs. Abdul to watch over Grandmommy.

Tola and Moji and Dapo struggle along until they reach the place on the Ikorodu Road where Grandmommy sells groundnuts.

It is a good spot near an overpass that carries many-many lanes of traffic to other parts of the city. Under the overpass a mechanic repairs cars.

Moji lights the fire and stirs the groundnuts.

Tola shouts, "Groundnut! Grooooooundnut!"

Dapo is supposed to be twisting newspaper into cones, but he has wandered off to watch the mechanic.

All day long Tola and Moji feed the fire and pour roasted groundnuts into newspaper twists and shout to customers. All day long they count out change and chase after cars with people

holding their money out of open windows.

Night comes. The hawkers light their kerosene lamps, the traffic becomes a stream of blinding lights, and the mechanic locks up his yard and leaves.

Moji stands up with a groan. Tola counts their money. And Dapo reappears.

"We have only enough for half a loaf of bread and one tin of sardines tonight," Tola says.

Dapo wails.

"I am more hungry than that!" he says.

"We must save money to buy more groundnuts and oil for tomorrow," Tola says.

"But Grandmommy always makes more than that!" Dapo complains.

"We would have made more if you had worked too," Moji growls.

Dapo stops complaining and hangs his head.

Tola and Dapo and Moji walk home, stopping only at the night market to buy one tin of sardines and half a loaf of bread.

It is not enough to stop them from feeling very-very hungry.

Back in their room, Grandmommy is still sweating. She is moaning. Her eyes are still closed.

"She will improve," Mrs. Abdul says gently. "She will improve."

But by morning she has not improved. So instead of packing up their pencils and books, the children go out to work in the hot sun.

Moji's throat is sore from breathing in the fumes from the fire.

Tola's throat is sore from calling after customers.

Dapo's throat is not sore at all. He has gone to watch the cars being repaired, and no amount of shouting brings him back.

Day after day it is the same. Grandmommy is sick. And they have to work, not go to school.

Then one night they get back to their room and Tola hears voices. One of them is Grandmommy's!

"Grandmommy!" Tola shouts, and rushes in.

Grandmommy is lying on the bed talking to Mrs. Abdul. She looks weak but she smiles. And then she frowns.

"What is this?" She waves her hand weakly at the loads on their heads.

Tola and Dapo and Moji look at one another.

Grandmommy narrows her eyes. "Were you selling groundnuts?" she hisses.

"We were hungry!" Tola whispers.

"School, nko?" Grandmommy asks.

Moji and Dapo and Tola look at their feet.

Grandmommy frowns even harder.

"We needed money," Moji whispers.

"Moji, you knew there was money," Grandmommy says.

Moji opens her mouth. Then she closes it again.

"Moji." Grandmommy suddenly looks worried. "Moji, what of my money?"

"We bought medicine," Moji whispers.

"For you!" Dapo says hopefully.

"Medicine!" Grandmommy is horrified. "Medicine! How much did you spend?"

They all look back down at their feet. Tola can hear her heart pounding like feet running away.

"How much?" Grandmommy whispers. "How much did you spend?"

Tola and Moji and Dapo cannot speak. Their mouths have dried up like ponds before the rainy season. Their tongues, like dead fish, refuse to move.

"How much?" Grandmommy whispers again.

"All," says Moji, crying.

Grandmommy slumps back in the bed.

"I am bankrupt! Bankrupt! These good-for-nothing children have bankrupted me-o! And for what? For unnecessary medicine!"

"Nonsense," Mrs. Abdul says loudly. "You would have died without that medicine."

"Died!" Grandmommy protests. "Who are you calling dead? I lay down yesterday and I will get up tomorrow."

Mrs. Abdul sucks her teeth.

"Mama Mighty, you have been lying there for almost two weeks!" she snaps.

"Two weeks!" Grandmommy sits up again, looking horrified. "Two weeks!"

She looks at Tola and Moji and Dapo again.

"You have been managing alone for two weeks," she whispers.

Then she holds her arms out to them.

"Come here," she says.

Tola and Dapo and Moji rush into Grandmommy's arms. *It feels like home,* Tola thinks.

Next morning Grandmommy is still too weak to get out of bed. But she takes charge.

"This morning," she says, "Moji must go to school!"

Moji claps her hands happily. She has missed her lessons. She has missed the quiet. She has missed her friends. And she has missed the air-conditioning!

"Tola and Dapo, you must go to work now before you miss the morning customers," Grandmommy continues.

Tola stares at Grandmommy. Grandmommy looks at her sadly. Tola loves school too. Grandmommy knows that!

"But what of me?" Tola whispers.

"Your school is not like Moji's," Grandmommy says sadly. "It does not guarantee you a job. And if Moji loses her scholarship at her fine-fine school, then we will always be struggling to eat."

"Sorry, Tola," Moji whispers.

Tola turns away. She loads the pans on her

head without a word. Dapo does not complain. But he does not help either. When they get to their place on the Ikorodu Road, he wanders off to the mechanic's.

"Dapo!" Tola shouts as she counts out change for a customer.

The groundnuts need turning but Dapo has his head in the hood of a car.

"Dapo!" Tola wails as she frantically pours nuts into newspaper.

The fire needs fanning but Dapo is underneath a car.

"Dapo!" Tola screams as someone waves for groundnuts from the window of their car.

The groundnuts are burning but Dapo is learning how to weld bits of cars onto other cars.

At the end of the day, Tola marches toward the overpass. The mechanics are lounging on the cars. And there is Dapo, smiling and joking with them!

Tola marches right up behind him.

"You call yourself my brother?" she shouts.

Dapo jumps. He jumps high enough to touch the ears of a giraffe.

"What brother would let his small sister work alone while he plays around with these useless machines!"

Tola waves her hands at the cars. Dapo looks as if he wants a trunk to open and swallow him up.

"She is small . . ." one of the mechanics mutters.

"But she is mighty," whispers another.

"Like the grandmother," hisses the boss.

Tola puffs herself up like an angry lizard, ready to continue her tirade. But a shiny SUV

pulls up under the overpass. A window opens
and a woman leans out.

"I need somebody to fix my car!" she shouts.

The mechanics are still frozen by Tola's
shouting. It is Dapo who defrosts first. He runs
toward the SUV.

"Madam, madam, how can we help you?"
he calls.

"My car is not working." The woman is panicking.

"What is wrong with the car?"

It is the boss speaking to the woman now. She explains fast.

"It sounds like the clutch," the boss says. "You need a new one."

"Please," the woman begs. "Install a new one now so that I can get my children home."

"Sorry, madam—" the boss says.

"I will pay double if you can do it now," the woman interrupts.

The boss's eyes widen, and for a moment he looks like a small child alone with a big cake. He has to screw his eyes up tightly to speak.

"I am sorry, madam," he says again.

Dapo tugs the boss's arm. He whispers in his ear. The boss's face changes. He smiles broadly.

"Madam," he says. "Of course. Do not worry. You have come to the right place. Soon your car will be purring like a leopard."

"Boss," one of the other mechanics whispers. "We have no—"

"This boy can make one fit," the boss interrupts.

Tola sucks her teeth. She waits and waits. Then she sighs and squats down to wait. She waits a long time.

By the time Dapo is finished, rush hour is over, the traffic is moving quickly, and the SUV works just fine!

A fat roll of money passes from the hands of the grateful woman into the boss's shirt.

"Thank you! Thank you!" she shouts. "I will come back. And I will send all my friends here!"

The mechanics throw Dapo up into the air and cheer. Then the boss whispers in his ear.

"Dapo!" Tola shouts. She has had enough!

"He is coming! He is coming-o!" The boss pats Dapo's back.

Tola loads the pans back onto her head. She leaves the brazier for Dapo.

"Grandmommy is going to kill you for making us so late."

Dapo says nothing. He is smiling. All the way

home he smiles. Tola sucks her teeth.

"Wait until Grandmommy gets hold of you," she says.

Dapo still says nothing. Not until he steps through their door.

"Nobody in this family," he says then, "is going to sell groundnuts anymore."

Grandmommy's mouth was open, ready to shout, but now she frowns instead. Moji looks up from her books.

"What did you say?" Grandmommy growls.

"Nobody in this family," Dapo says again, "is going to sell groundnuts anymore."

"What are you talking about?" Grandmommy frowns.

Dapo takes some money out of his pocket and gives it to Grandmommy.

"This is my today's wages!" he says.

Grandmommy's eyes open wide. Tola gasps. Moji splutters.

"Selling groundnuts?" Grandmommy chokes. "You earned all of this selling groundnuts?"

"Noooo." Dapo laughs. "I am useless at selling groundnuts. I earned it fixing cars!"

"Cars!" Grandmommy splutters.

"Yes," Dapo announces. "I have a job. I am going to work every Monday to Saturday. And I will be paid this amount every single day!"

Grandmommy stares at the money. It is more than she earns in a good week!

Grandmommy looks at Dapo. She shakes her head. She blinks hard. She clears her throat.

"I have been wrong about you," she croaks. "You are not useless, Dapo."

Dapo grins.

"No, Grandmommy," he says. "You were right. I am useless at school. I am useless at housework. I am useless at selling groundnuts. But when it comes to cars—then I am mighty too!"

Grandmommy laughs. And Moji laughs.

And Tola laughs too.

Dapo looks at Tola.

"Tola," he says, "tomorrow you can go back to school."

Tola looks at Grandmommy. Grandmommy smiles and nods her head.

Tola jumps up and down and claps her hands and dances around the room. The pots and pans fall off her head, and everybody laughs.

Tola laughs again too. Grandmommy is better, Dapo has a job, and tomorrow—tomorrow—tomorrow she is going back to school!

Tola and the Three Fine Girls

Tola lives in a run-down block of apartments in the megacity of Lagos, in the country of Nigeria. In the city of Lagos, there are girls who have their own beds, girls who have their own bathrooms, girls who have their own cars and their own drivers to drive them. Then there are girls who do not. And Tola is one of those.

Tola is on her way home from market with Grandmommy. They have bought sweet corn, they have bought goat meat, they have bought all kinds of fine-fine food because now Dapo has a job and they can afford to eat well-well.

Tola is excited because today is masquerade day in Lagos. Tall figures with scary masks will dance in the city streets. They will twirl and whirl slowly to drums. And people will crowd to see them!

"Grandmommy, can I go?" Tola pleads as they walk home from the market. "Please, I beg you!"

Grandmommy sucks her teeth.

"Who will you go with?" she asks.

Tola looks at Grandmommy. Grandmommy raises her eyebrows.

"You see my feet?"

Tola looks down at Grandmommy's feet. They are so swollen they are bulging out of her flip-flops. Grandmommy's feet need to rest!

"How about Moji?" asks Tola hopefully.

Grandmommy snorts. "You have the power to drag your sister from her homework?" she asks.

Tola purses her lips.

"Dapo!" Tola exclaims.

Grandmommy shakes her head, exasperated.

"Your brother works hard, and by the time he gets home he is only fit to eat and sleep."

Tola nods sadly. It was true. Sometimes Dapo was so tired he fell asleep while eating.

"Maybe I could go by myself?" Tola says quickly.

Grandmommy says nothing. And nothing means *No*. Tola sighs loudly. Grandmommy ignores her. They cross the road to where the fancy shops are.

"Mama Mighty!" somebody calls out to Grandmommy.

Grandmommy stops. The man calling her is the uncle of her cousin's cousin. Grandmommy smiles. She will enjoy catching up on all the family news.

Tola stands on one foot. And then on the other foot. She does not enjoy standing outside fancy shops. She has never been inside any of those shops. They are too expensive and too cold. And everybody around is too-too fine. They make Tola feel she is not so good. But Grandmommy and the uncle talk and talk. So Tola looks into one of the shop windows.

She stares at the sneakers. Sharp blue sneakers, smart black sneakers, cute pink sneakers, sporty yellow sneakers, cool red sneakers . . .

Tola looks down at her own dusty worn-out flip-flops. She would like to wear a pair of new sneakers! But when she looks at the price tags, she gasps. Those sneakers cost more than five times Grandmommy's malaria medicine!

Tola turns away from the window. A girl is walking toward her. A girl wearing a pink skirt and a T-shirt embroidered with a silver heart. A woman wearing big sunglasses and carrying a handbag is walking next to the girl. Neither of them notice Tola. She is too shabby to be noticeable.

"Mama?" the girl says to the woman.

Her mother does not answer. She is too busy talking into her phone.

"Mama?" the girl asks again.

"What is it?" her mother snaps at her impatiently.

The girl points to the sneakers in the shop window. And without saying one word, her mother pulls money out of her handbag and hands it to her daughter.

While the girl is in the shop, the woman continues talking. "We will come to the masquerade," she says, "but not until later on. I have a lot to do today."

The girl comes out wearing cute pink sneakers that match her skirt and T-shirt.

"Look, Mama!" she says.

Her mother looks but she continues to talk on her phone. The girl bites her lip.

Tola thinks it is a shame that the woman did not notice how fine her daughter looked. And she thinks it is a shame to look so sad when one looks so fine.

Tola looks at Grandmommy. Grandmommy
is telling a long story about the business partner
that her cousin had in Ibadan years ago.

Tola knows better than to interrupt
Grandmommy. In Nigeria children are taught
never to interrupt.

So instead she looks into the window of a
shop selling blue jeans. There are dark jeans
the color of indigo and light jeans the color
of harmattan skies. There are even jeans that

sparkle with
diamonds!

Tola looks
down at her
own jeans.
They are too
short and too
loose, and the
stains make
them look dirty.

A girl Tola's age comes out of the shop. She is wearing a pair of jeans as faded as Tola's. But her jeans fit her all the way up and all the way

down. And they have no stains at all.

Tola stares at the girl. Her jeans are cool. Her denim jacket is cool. Her hair that falls down her back like a black waterfall looks freshly done and cool, cool, cool! And her hands clutch shopping bags with cool logos like Adidas and Apple.

A car horn beeps loudly and a BMW with blacked-out windows pulls up.

"Daddy!" the girl cries, and rushes to the car.

A uniformed man puts his head out of the driver's window.

"Your father sent me to collect you," the man says.

The girl stops in her tracks.

"Is he at home?" she asks hopefully.

"He is busy in the office," the man says. "He will not be home until late."

The girl slumps into the back of the car with her shopping bags. Her eyes and mouth point downward. Tola thinks it is a shame to look so disappointed when one has so many cool things. Tola sighs.

Grandmommy looks at Tola.

"O-ya," Grandmommy says, "let's go!"

Tola does not hear her. She is staring at a girl wearing a traditional buba and iro in matching bright-red cloth with white airplanes printed on it. The girl's hair is styled traditionally too. It is

wound round and round
with black thread and bent
into curved shapes all over
her head.

Tola touches her rough hair in
its thick braids. She sighs again.

Grandmommy comes to stand
right in front of Tola.

"What is the matter with you?"
she asks.

"Nothing, Grandmommy," Tola lies.

"Nothing?" Grandmommy asks. "Is that why
you are sighing every two minutes?"

"I just wish . . ." Tola stops.

She knows Grandmommy will not
understand.

"Wish for what?" Grandmommy asks. "Wish
for what?"

"I wish I was as fine as all these girls," Tola
says at last.

"Fine?" Grandmommy asks. "Why do you need to be fine? Do you not have a roof over your head?"

"Yes, Grandmommy," Tola says slowly.

"And do you not have more than enough food to eat?"

"Yes, Grandmommy," Tola says more slowly.

"And are you not able to go to school?"

"Yes, Grandmommy," Tola says even more slowly.

"So why do you need to be fine?" Grandmommy asks impatiently.

"Because . . ." Tola says, "because . . ." But what Tola feels does not match any of the words she knows.

"Exactly! Because nothing!" says Grandmommy. "Let's go."

Tola follows Grandmommy. She tries not to cry. Grandmommy looks at her out of the corner of her eye. Tola does not notice.

As soon as they get home, Grandmommy says to Moji, "O-ya! Time to start cooking."

Moji looks up from her homework. She frowns one of her A+ scholarship frowns.

"Who do you think you are looking at like that?" Grandmommy asks crossly.

Moji lowers her eyes.

"Maybe you have forgotten how to cook?" Grandmommy asks.

"No, Grandmommy," Moji says, but her eyes are back on her computer screen.

"So what are you waiting for?" Grandmommy bellows.

Moji jumps up. She rushes to gather onions and tomatoes. Tola helps. There are onions to chop and tomatoes to grind and fish to fry.

"Tola," Grandmommy says, "leave that. Loose your hair and go and wash it."

Tola and Moji stare at Grandmommy. It is not hair-washing day! Saturday is hair-washing day.

"Can you not hear me?" Grandmommy frowns.

"Sorry, Grandmommy!" Tola says.

Quickly Tola starts to loosen her hair. And quickly Moji goes back to chopping onions. Nobody wants Grandmommy to bellow again.

Tola's hair is divided into neat sections and braided into thick braids. It is all that anyone has time or money for.

Quickly Tola loosens the thick braids. Then she hurries down the outside corridor to the bathroom with a bucket, a jug, a towel, and a bar of soap.

In the bathroom there are two taps. One should be hot and one should be cold. They are both cold.

Tola fills up the bucket with cold water. She bends forward and carefully pours jugfuls of water over her head. When it is completely wet, she soaps her hair thoroughly. When she has finished soaping, she uses the rest of the water in the bucket to rinse her hair. Then she hurries back with the towel wrapped around her head.

Back in their room, Grandmommy is looking tired. She has kicked off her tight shoes and is stretching her swollen feet. But she has a comb and a jar of Vaseline on her wide lap.

"O-ya, sit," Grandmommy says to Tola, gesturing to the floor in front of her.

Tola hesitates. On Saturday Moji always braids Tola's hair into thick braids. Why is Grandmommy going to do it today?

"What is wrong with you children?" Grandmommy asks again crossly. "Do I have to say everything twice?"

Tola quickly sits on the floor in between Grandmommy's knees. She decides not to risk asking any questions.

Grandmommy takes the comb. She combs out Tola's hair. It is so thick and so curly that it takes some time.

Grandmommy parts Tola's hair in half and ties one half out of the way. And then she parts the remainder in half and ties the other half out of the way. Tola waits for her to braid the remaining quarter into a big thick braid. But she does not.

No, now Grandmommy divides a tiny section off from the remaining quarter neatly with the comb. She ties the big section out of the way. And then she starts to weave the remaining section into a tiny, tiny, tiny braid.

Tola's eyes open wide, wide, wide!

Once upon a time, Grandmommy used to weave braids tinier and neater and finer than anybody else in the apartments. That was before her hands became thick and old and tired from cooking groundnuts for a living.

Moji is staring at the teeny tiny braids that Grandmommy is weaving on Tola's head.

"Do you think we will eat today?" Grandmommy asks her. "Or will you still be standing there until midnight?"

Moji drags her eyes away from Tola's head and goes back to chopping onions and grinding tomatoes.

For three whole hours, Grandmommy braids teeny tiny strands of Tola's hair together. For three whole hours, she bends Tola's aching neck backward and forward and side to side. Tola's scalp stings as Grandmommy pulls fingerfuls of hair into braids. But Tola does not complain. Oh no! She is having her hair weaved for the first time in her life—she has nothing whatsoever to complain about!

"Grandmommy?" Tola dares to ask after some time has passed.

Grandmommy grunts in answer.

"Did you use to weave Mama's hair?"

For one second Grandmommy's fingers stop. And so do Moji's. Then Grandmommy starts to weave again.

"I braided your mother's hair every week when she was your age," Grandmommy says.

And then Grandmommy tells them stories of how their mother used to demand a different hairstyle every week.

"She loved to follow the fashion." Grandmommy sighs.

"Was she fine?" Tola asks.

"Of course!" Grandmommy says. "She was the most beautiful girl in the whole of Lagos."

Tola and Moji both sigh as Grandmommy weaves both braids and stories of their mother. She makes a crisscross pattern all over Tola's head.

Suddenly Grandmommy stops.

"Get my box from under the bed," she says. "The Dove one."

Tola gets up on aching legs. Grandmommy rummages inside the box. She brings out a plastic bag. Inside the bag are beads. Shiny, glittering beads.

Tola's eyes shine as brightly as the beads!

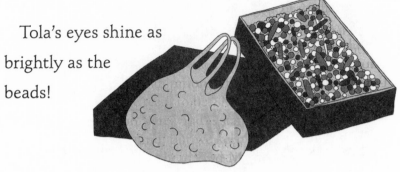

And one by one by one Grandmommy braids the beads into her hair. Tola can feel each braid becoming heavier under the weight of each bead. She cannot believe how lucky she is!

At last Grandmommy smears cool Vaseline in between each braid, and Tola's tight and aching scalp is soothed. Then Grandmommy pats her head.

"Finish," she says.

Tola scrambles up and runs to the broken mirror propped against the wall. She gasps!

Her whole head is covered with tiny interweaving braids, and near the end of each braid a glittering bead sparkles. Tola moves and her whole head shimmers.

Moji claps her hands. "Tola, you are so fine!"
she exclaims.

Tola cannot stop looking in the mirror. And
she cannot stop smiling. She does look so fine.
She has never looked so fine in her life before!

Behind her in the mirror Tola can see
Grandmommy sitting with her swollen feet
resting on the floor and her swollen hands
resting in her lap. Even her tired eyes look
swollen.

Suddenly Tola turns around.
She goes to Grandmommy
and kneels
down. This
is the polite
way in
Nigeria.

"Thank you, Grandmommy," Tola says with all her heart.

She does not know if she is saying thank you for the braids or stories or thank you, Grandmommy, for braiding her hair even when it pains her hands. Maybe love and stories and braids are the same thing anyway.

Grandmommy smiles at Tola with shining eyes.

"You look as fine as your mother," she says.

And Tola's eyes shine too!

"I have to go and get more gari," Moji interrupts.

"Tola can go to ask Mrs. Abdul," Grandmommy says, patting Tola's cheek.

Tola jumps up. She can't wait to show Mrs. Abdul her hair.

In the corridor Tola passes Mrs. Shaky-Shaky.

"Beautiful!" Mrs. Shaky-Shaky puts a shaky hand to Tola's hair.

"Thank you!" Tola smiles shyly.

The sound of voices makes Mama Business open her door. She stares at Tola's hair.

"Mama Mighty is braiding again?" she asks.

Before even waiting for Tola to answer, Mama Business is knocking on doors.

"Mama Mighty is braiding again!" she announces at each one.

She even manages to get to Mrs. Abdul's door before Tola does.

"Come and look!" she shouts.

Mrs. Abdul puts out her head. When she sees Tola, she claps her hands too.

"Tola!" she says. "Fine-fine girl!"

Tola beams.

Mr. Abdul the tailor pokes his head out too.

"Tola!" he exclaims when he sees her. "You will be the finest girl at the masquerade!"

Tola's smile shrinks small.

"I am not going," she says.

"Why?" Mr. Abdul cries. "You cannot miss it!"

"Grandmommy's feet are too swollen. Moji is studying. And Dapo is working," Tola says. "I have nobody to take me." She shrugs. "It is OK. I will go next year."

Mr. Abdul looks at Mrs. Abdul. Mrs. Abdul smiles and nods. And she nods again when Tola asks for gari.

Mr. Abdul walks with Tola back to her room.

"Salam alekum," Mr. Abdul says as he enters.

"Peace be with you too, Mr. Abdul," Grandmommy replies. "How is your family today?"

"We are all well, *hamdulillah*," Mr. Abdul says. "How are you and the children today?"

"We too are well, praise God!" Grandmommy replies.

"Today is the masquerade . . ." Mr. Abdul begins.

"I know, I know." Grandmommy sighs.

"I love the masquerade," Mr. Abdul continues, "but Mrs. Abdul does not want to take baby Jide out into the crowds."

"She is very wise," Grandmommy agrees. "Crowds are not good for babies."

"So I must go alone," Mr. Abdul says mournfully. "And it is not so good to go to the masquerade alone. It is better to go with a friend. So that you and your friend can discuss everything that you see together."

Grandmommy grunts.

"I understand," Tola says. "If I was going to the masquerade, I would want to go with a friend too."

Mr. Abdul smiles at her. Then he looks at Grandmommy. "If Tola comes with me, I would not have to go alone," he says.

Tola opens her eyes wide and holds her breath.

Grandmommy snorts. Then she smiles.

"Off you go," she says. "Mr. Abdul will look after you."

Tola jumps up and down. The shining beads bounce and sparkle! Mr. Abdul laughs.

"O-ya!" he says. "Let's go! Let us not miss anything!"

Tola and Mr. Abdul hurry out of the apartments.

Mr. Abdul gets on his big black bicycle. That bicycle is an old friend of Tola's.

Once she rode around the whole city on the back of it, taking measurements for Mr. Abdul, who makes clothes for the people of Lagos.

Tola jumps onto the luggage rack. And Mr.

Abdul pedals off. Like everyone in Lagos, Tola is so strong and her balance is so good she does not even need to hold on.

They ride down busy streets and bump down alleyways and sail over overpasses until they come to Surulere, the part of the city where the masquerade is happening.

All the way there, Tola can feel the shining beads on the ends of her beautiful braids bounce up and down. It feels like the love of her grandmother. It feels like the memory of her mother. Tola could sail all the way to Surulere on her happiness.

"Can you see the masquerade dancers, Tola? Can you see them?" Mr. Abdul shouts when they get there.

"No!" Tola shouts back.

The streets are crowded now. And all Tola can see are the backs of people in the crowd. But she can hear the drumming. And people shouting.

The masquerade must be so close!

"Climb up!" Mr. Abdul shouts. "Climb up to see!"

So Tola stands up on the back of the bike rack with one hand on Mr. Abdul's shoulder. Mr. Abdul pedals the bike between some cars. The cars cannot get any closer.

Suddenly Tola can see!

The dancers with their carved-wood faces move slowly to the fast-beating drums. They circle and bend and bow. And their long, heavy costumes sway from side to side.

"I see dem!" Tola shouts. "I see dem!"

In the cars a group of girls hears Tola shout. One is wearing a pink outfit. One is wearing skinny jeans. And one is wearing red cloth printed with white airplanes.

All three girls stare at Tola standing upright on the back of a bicycle. She is laughing and pointing and her hair sparkles around her face like a star!

"I wish I was allowed to ride around the city on the back of a bicycle," says the girl in the pink sneakers.

"I wish I could see the masquerade," says the girl in skinny jeans.

"I don't care about the masquerade," says the girl in the red cloth. "I just wish I was as happy as that fine-fine girl."

"Me too," says the girl in the pink sneakers.

The three girls look at Tola shining and they all sigh. Tola looks like the happiest girl in the world . . .

And that is exactly how she feels!